cloverleaf books™

Alike and Different

My Family, Your Family

Lisa Bullard

illustrated by **Renée Kurilla**

M MILLBROOK PRESS · MINNEAPOLIS

Dedicated to AMAZE, an organization committed to creating a world where all families are valued and respected. Special thanks to AMAZE Executive Director Nancy Michael for her insightful feedback, which added immensely to this title.
—L.B.

For my own family, whose cozy homes and impeccable landscaping skills inspired the pages of this book. I love each and every one of you.
—R.K.

Millbrook Press
A division of Lerner Publishing Group, Inc.
241 First Avenue North
Minneapolis, MN 55401 USA

For reading levels and more information, look up this title at www.lernerbooks.com.

Main body text set in Slappy Inline 18/28.
Typeface provided by T26.

Library of Congress Cataloging-in-Publication Data

Bullard, Lisa.
    My family, your family / by Lisa Bullard ; illustrated by Renée Kurilla.
        pages   cm. — (Cloverleaf books™ : alike and different)
    Includes index.
    ISBN 978-1-4677-4901-5 (lib. bdg. : alk. paper) —
ISBN 978-1-4677-6029-4 (PB) — ISBN 978-1-4677-6292-2 (EB pdf)
    1. Families—Juvenile literature. 2. Households—Juvenile literature. I. Title.
HQ744.B77 2015
306.85—dc23   2014015147

Manufactured in the United States of America
10 - 50942 - 17025 - 8/24/2021

TABLE OF CONTENTS

Chapter One

A Treasure Hunt

I'm Makayla. Did you know that I have the best family ever? It's true! This is my mom and dad. This is our dog, Tootsie. We all really love ice cream. But we love each other even more.

Did you notice Mom's belly? She's going to have a baby soon. The doctor says it will be a brother. I'm worried that will **change everything.**

This morning, Mom and Dad have a plan. They agree the baby will make our family different. But Mom says that **different can be great.**

6

So I'm spending time with other families. Dad tells me to find one great thing about each different family.

It's like a treasure hunt!

A family might be people related by birth, adoption, or marriage. Or it might be people who love and take care of one another. Some family members live together. Some family members live apart. Who is in your family?

I'm at Mateo's house for breakfast. He lives with his mom and dad, like me. **But his family is bigger and noisier.** Mateo's three sisters talk a lot. And everybody talks loudly so that Mateo's grandpa can hear. They call him *abuelo*. That's the Spanish word for grandfather.

My mom was right that different can be a good thing. Mateo's family is so fun! There's always someone to play with.

Different families speak different languages at home. What language do you use with your family?

Chapter Two

Other Kinds of Families

Next, I take a walk with Ms. Betsy and Ms. Roberta. They live together across the street. I thought you had to have kids to be a family. But **Mom says all you need to be a family is love.**

My ears are worn out after my loud breakfast. So Ms. Betsy and Ms. Roberta let me do the talking. Here's a great thing about their family. They really know how to make other people feel important!

I eat lunch with Olivia and her dad. Olivia's parents are divorced. Olivia stays with her dad on weekends. Her mom lives in another part of town.

I don't know much about divorce. But I can see that Olivia's dad loves her. And she tells me that her mom and stepdad and stepsister do too. Olivia's family is pretty awesome.

She has **two** homes where she belongs!

Sometimes after a divorce, a child's parent marries someone else. This person is called a stepparent. if the stepparent already has children, the child also gains stepbrothers or stepsisters.

Chapter Three
Families Take Care of You

After lunch, I visit Jake's family. His grandma and grandpa take care of him. Grandma helps us bake Jake's **favorite cookies.** Grandpa shows us how to build a shelf.

Jake's grandparents have had lots of years to learn cool stuff. So they're really good at teaching Jake new things!

Next, I visit Parker's family. **He's adopted.**
Parker tells me his mother loved him, but she
couldn't take care of him. And Parker's two dads
knew he was meant to be their little boy.

Here's what's special about Parker's family. His dad works during the day. Then his papa works at night. So he always has a dad around to take care of him!

Some children who are adopted were born in the United States. Some were born in other countries. Either way, their adoptive families feel like they were meant to be together.

When I get home, **my family is bigger.** No, the baby isn't here yet! Gramp and Grammy came for dinner. And Nana and Uncle Monty flew in a plane to see us.

Aunt Jean and my three cousins are here too. Aunt Jean's the only grown-up in their family, unless the cats count. So I know what makes their family great. **Everybody does their part to help out!**

Chapter Four

Different Can Be Great

I'm sleepy. Mom and Dad and Tootsie tuck me in. Mom says my baby brother can hear my voice from her belly. So I tell him about all the families I met today.

I know different can be great. Having a brother will change our family. But we'll still love him more than ice cream!

Make a "One Great Thing" Poster

If Makayla visited your family, what great things would she find? Make a list. Ask the other people in your family for their ideas too.

Pick one of your family's great things and make a poster about that thing. Add pictures if you want to. Hang it somewhere for everyone in your family to see.

Here are some examples:

1) My family loves each other more than ice cream!

2) There is always somebody to play with in my family.

3) My family makes me feel important.

4) My family takes care of me.

5) My family was meant to be together.

6) Everybody does their part in my family.

GLOSSARY

abuelo: the Spanish word for "grandfather"

adopted: a child who has been especially chosen to be part of a family even though they were not born into that family

aunt: your father's or mother's sister, or the female partner of an aunt or uncle

cousin: your aunt's or uncle's child

divorced: not married anymore, after a couple officially ends their marriage

nana: another name for grandmother

stepdad: a parent's marriage partner who is not the child's original father

stepsister: a girl child of a stepparent

uncle: your father's or mother's brother, or the male partner of an aunt or uncle

BOOKS

Hoffman, Mary. *The Great Big Book of Families.* New York: Dial, 2011.
You can learn more about all different sorts of families in this fun-filled book.

Kuklin, Susan. *Families.* New York: Hyperion, 2006.
Meet many different real-life kids and find out what it's like to be a part of their families.

WEBSITES

PBS Kids Go!: Sibling Rivalry
http://pbskids.org/itsmylife/video/index.html?guid=88b942dd-1010-41c7-9629-e0b0aacba8cb
Watch a video to see how other kids get along with their brother or sister.

Women's and Children's Health Network: Your Family
http://www.cyh.com/HealthTopics/HealthTopicCategories.aspx?p=282
This website answers a long list of questions that you might have about families.

LERNER SOURCE™
Expand learning beyond the printed book. Download free, complementary educational resources for this book from our website, www.lerneresource.com.